BIG GIRL
IN THE
BIG WORLD

Hello, the little dreamer!

Let's spark, embrace, and dream together!

Chloe Felix, a beloved author, brings joy to children with her engaging books. Her work inspires and ignites children's boundless imaginations and promotes skills development through delightful and educational content, nurturing a love for learning, creativity, and positive values.

Table of Contents

Introduction

Big Girl in the Big World is a heartwarming collection of inspiring stories, meticulously crafted to embolden and empower young readers as they navigate the vast and often daunting world. Each story in this beautifully curated anthology shines a light on the incredible journey of self-discovery, bravery, and the unyielding power of love. From tales of girls who dared to dream big and bravely challenge the norms, to narratives of inner strength overcoming life's obstacles, this book is a testament to the indomitable spirit that is innate in every young girl.

These stories are carefully woven with themes of self-confidence and courage, designed to resonate with readers on a personal level. They portray heroines from a variety of back-grounds and circumstances, each finding her unique path to triumph and happiness. The **Big Girl in the Big World** not only entertains but also instills confidence, igniting a spark of determination and hope in the hearts of its readers.

Whether it's about making a difference in the community, standing up against adversity, or even the path to self-love and acceptance, these stories are a great celebration of the extraordinary potential within every young girl. **Big Girl in the Big World** invites its readers to embark on an inspiring and exceptional journey of discovery, fostering belief in their abilities and the magic they can create in the big world.

Emily and the Enchanted Forest

Learning is like going on an endless adventure where you discover new things every day. It's not just about books and school, but about being curious and asking lots of questions about everything around you. Every day is a chance to learn something cool and exciting. So, keep your eyes open, stay curious, and don't be afraid to ask "why?" or "how?" Remember, the more you learn, the more amazing things you can do.

Once upon a time, in a cozy little town surrounded by majestic mountains and lush forests, lived a bright-eyed girl named Emily. Emily was ten years old, with a curious mind and an adventurous spirit. She loved to explore, to ask questions, and to learn about the world around her.

Emily lived with her parents and her little brother, Tommy, in a small house at the edge of the town. Their home was special, as it sat right next to a vast, mysterious forest that the townsfolk called the Enchanted Forest. It was said that the forest was full of wonders and secrets, a place where magical things happened to those who dared to explore it.

One sunny Saturday morning, Emily decided she would venture into the Enchanted Forest. She wanted to see if the stories were true, and more importantly, she wanted to learn about the plants, animals, and mysteries the forest held.

"Don't go too far, Emily," her mother warned, "and be back before dinner."

"I will, Mom!" Emily said, tying her shoelaces. She grabbed her backpack, filled with a notebook, a pencil, a small magnifying glass, and a bottle of water.

As Emily stepped into the forest, she felt a rush of excitement. The trees were tall and majestic, their leaves whispering secrets in the wind. Sunlight danced through the branches, creating patterns on the forest floor. It was more beautiful than she had ever imagined.

Emily started her exploration, jotting down notes and sketches of different plants and insects she found. She observed a line of ants carrying food, a spider weaving its web, and a variety of colorful birds singing in the treetops.

Deep in the forest, Emily stumbled upon a small clearing. In the center stood a grand old oak tree, its branches reaching high into the sky. It was the biggest tree she had ever seen.

"This must be the Guardian of the Forest," Emily whispered to herself, remembering a story her grandmother had told her. She approached the tree and gently placed her hand on its trunk. The tree's bark was warm, and it felt almost like it was humming a soft melody.

"Hello, Emily," a voice said.

Startled, Emily looked around. To her amazement, the voice had come from the oak tree.

"Don't be afraid," the tree continued. "I am the Guardian of this forest. I have been watching over it for hundreds of years."

Emily's eyes widened with wonder. "Can you talk to all the creatures in the forest?"

"Yes, I can," the tree replied. "And I have much to teach you. But remember, the greatest lessons come from observing and listening."

The Guardian told Emily about the forest, the delicate balance of nature, the importance of every plant and animal, and how they all depended on each other. Emily listened intently, her notebook quickly filling with notes and sketches.

As the sun began to set, the Guardian spoke, "It's time for you to return home, Emily. But you are always welcome here."

"Thank you, Guardian," Emily said, her heart full of gratitude. "I'll come back to learn more."

True to her word, Emily visited the Enchanted Forest every weekend. Each visit was a new adventure. She learned about medicinal plants, the language of birds, the secrets of the old trees, and the tiny insects that played a big role in the health of the forest.

Emily shared her knowledge with her friends and family. She told them about the importance of preserving nature, of being kind to the environment, and of the endless wonders that the natural world held.

As the years passed, Emily grew into a wise and kind young woman, known in the town for her love of nature and her vast knowledge about the Enchanted Forest. She took care of the forest, planting new trees, and ensuring it remained a safe haven for all its creatures.

One day, Emily received news that developers were planning to cut down a part of the Enchanted Forest to build new houses.

Heartbroken, Emily knew she had to do something. She organized a town meeting and spoke passionately about the importance of the forest, its beauty, and its role in their lives.

"Every plant, every animal in that forest is a part of our world," Emily told the townsfolk. "We must protect it, for it teaches us about life, about balance, and about the beauty of nature."

Moved by Emily's words and her love for the forest, the townsfolk joined her in her effort to save it. Together, they petitioned, protested, and finally convinced the developers to leave the Enchanted Forest untouched.

The forest was saved, and Emily's actions inspired others to care for the environment. The Guardian of the Forest, proud of Emily's courage and wisdom, whispered, "You have learned well, and you have taught others. This is the greatest gift."

Emily continued to visit the Enchanted Forest, each time learning something new. She realized that learning was a lifelong journey, an adventure that never ended. She shared her knowledge with the younger generations, teaching them to respect, appreciate, and protect nature.

"Always be learning," Emily would say. "For in learning, we grow, we understand, and we make the world a better place."

And so, the Enchanted Forest remained, a magical place of learning and wonder, watched over by Emily and the Guardian, a testament to the power of curiosity, knowledge, and the enduring spirit of nature.

The End.

This story of Emily and the Enchanted Forest serves as a beautiful metaphor for the journey of learning and the importance of protecting our natural world. It inspires young girls to be curious, to seek knowledge, and to stand up for what they believe in.

Lila's Leap of Independence

To all the young girls out there: Being independent is super cool. It means making your own choices, believing in yourself, and not being afraid to try new things. Always remember, you can do anything you set your mind to. Don't wait for someone else to tell you what you can or can't do. Stand tall, be brave, and follow your heart. Every day is a new chance to show the world just how awesome and strong you are.

There was a young girl named Lila who lived in the heart of a bustling town, where streets buzzed with laughter and the air hummed with dreams. Lila, with her sparkly eyes and wild, curly hair, was not your ordinary girl. She was known for her adventurous spirit and her desire to forge her own path.

Lila lived with her loving parents, who always encouraged her to be independent. Her mother often said, "Lila, you have wings. Don't be afraid to fly." Her father would add, "And remember, independence isn't doing everything alone; it's knowing you can."

One sunny day, Lila decided to enter the town's annual "Young Inventors Fair." She had always been fascinated by how things worked and loved building gadgets from old toys and scrap materials. This year, she wanted to create something that would truly impress everyone, something that would symbolize her journey towards independence.

Lila spent days brainstorming ideas. She sketched and scribbled, thought and rethought. Finally, inspiration struck. She would build a mechanical bird that could fly! It was a challenging task, but Lila was ready for it.

She started working in her little makeshift workshop in the garage. Lila tinkered and toiled, assembling wings, adjusting gears, and programming the tiny robot brain she'd made. Each evening, she'd emerge with grease on her cheeks and excitement in her eyes.

Her parents watched her with pride, offering help and guidance when needed, but mostly they let Lila lead her project. They knew this was her chance to spread her wings.

As the day of the fair approached, Lila's mechanical bird – which she affectionately named "Sky" – was almost ready. However, during a test flight in her backyard, Sky suddenly whirred, sputtered, and crashed. Lila rushed to her fallen creation, her heart sinking. Sky was damaged, and the fair was just two days away.

Feeling defeated, Lila sat in the garage, staring at Sky's broken wing. She remembered her mother's words, "You have wings. Don't be afraid to fly." At that moment, Lila knew she couldn't give up. She had to try and fix Sky.

Working tirelessly, Lila repaired and repro-grammed Sky. It was hard work, and she en-countered many frustrating moments. But with each problem, Lila learned something new. She learned about resilience, about problem-solving, and most importantly, about trusting in her own abilities.

Finally, the big day arrived. Lila, with Sky safely tucked in her backpack, walked to the fair, her parents cheering her on. At the fair, there were so many incredible inventions by kids from all around town. Lila felt nervous but also excited to show Sky to the world.

When it was her turn, Lila placed Sky on the stage. The mechanical bird was a marvel. Lila explained how she built it, the challenges she faced, and how she overcame them. Then, with bated breath, she activated Sky.

Sky flapped its wings and soared! It glided above the audience, looping and twirling gracefully in the air. The crowd gasped in wonder and broke into applause. Lila beamed with pride. She had done it. She had brought her vision to life, and more importantly, she had done it independently.

Though Lila didn't win first place at the fair, she felt like a winner. She had tackled a challenge on her own, learned from her mistakes, and persevered. She had proven to herself that she could be independent, that she could solve problems and create solutions.

Back home, her parents hugged her tight. "You were spectacular," her mother said.

"You showed great independence today," her father added, "and that's the biggest win."

From that day on, Lila tackled life with even more vigor and independence. She knew that challenges would come, but she also knew that she had the strength and smarts to face them.

Years later, Lila became an accomplished inventor, known far and wide. And at every workshop or talk she gave, she always shared the story of Sky and the lesson she learned as a young girl: "Be independent. Trust in your abilities, learn from your challenges, and always, always believe in yourself."
gracefully in the air.

The End.

This story of Lila and her journey to build Sky, the mechanical bird, is designed to inspire young girls to embrace independence, face challenges with resilience, and believe in their capabilities. It illustrates the importance of self-belief and perseverance in the journey of personal growth.

Luna's True Melody

Hey girls! Always remember to be yourself. You are special just the way you are, with your own likes, dreams, and ideas. Don't worry about being like everyone else. Your own way is the best way for you. Like a puzzle piece, you fit perfectly into your own story. So, wear your favorite color, play your favorite game, and follow your heart. When you're true to yourself, you shine the brightest.

In the small, picturesque village of Melodyvale, where music flowed like a gentle river and every heart sang its own tune, lived a girl named Luna. Luna was twelve, with a smile that could light up the darkest nights and a laugh as clear as a bell. But deep down, Luna carried a secret – she felt out of tune with the world around her.

Melodyvale was famous for its musical talent. Every child seemed born to play an instrument, sing, or compose. Luna's family was no exception. Her father was a skilled violinist, her mother a gifted pianist, and her older brother a rising star with his guitar. They expected Luna to follow in their footsteps, to embrace the legacy of music that ran in her veins.

But Luna's heart danced to a different rhythm. She loved the stars. Luna was fascinated by the night sky, the constellations, and the stories they told. She had a telescope, through which she gazed at the cosmos, dreaming of distant galaxies and celestial wonders.

Luna tried to fit into Melodyvale's musical mold. She took piano lessons, tried singing, even attempted to compose music, but the notes felt like strangers, and her heart yearned for the stars.

One clear night, while Luna was stargazing, her grandmother, Mimi, joined her. "The stars are beautiful tonight," Mimi said softly.

"They are," Luna replied, her eyes not leaving the telescope.

"You don't seem happy playing music," Mimi observed.

Luna sighed, "I'm not, Mimi. I love astronomy. But everyone expects me to love music."

Mimi took Luna's hand, "Dear child, the music of your heart is yours alone. Be true to what sings within you. The stars are your melody."

Luna hugged her grandmother, tears of relief in her eyes. For the first time, she felt understood.

The next day, instead of practicing the piano, Luna decided to do something she had never done before. She set up her telescope in the village square, right next to the fountain where musicians often played.

Curious villagers gathered around as Luna pointed out constellations, shared facts about the planets, and told ancient stories written in the stars. Children and adults alike were mesmerized by Luna's passion and knowledge. She brought the universe to them, a melody of stars and space.

Luna's parents watched from a distance, surprised and moved by their daughter's courage and joy. They saw Luna in a new light, her eyes sparkling with excitement, her voice confident as she spoke about her love for astronomy.

From that day, Luna's passion for astronomy grew stronger as she delved deeper into her studies. She started a blog where she shared fascinating facts about the cosmos, breathtaking photos of celestial bodies, and her thoughts on the latest space explorations. Her blog, "Luna's Starry Sky," quickly gained popularity, attracting readers from all over the world.

Back in Melodyvale, Luna's astronomy club had become the talk of the town. Children who once only focused on music were now equally fascinated by the stars and planets. Luna's club was more than just a place to learn about astronomy; it was a place where children felt free to explore their interests, no matter how different they might be.

Luna's parents, seeing her dedication and the impact she was making, felt immense pride. They had realized that Luna's love for the stars was just as beautiful and important as their love for music. They encouraged her, providing her with books, telescopes, and even helped her organize a local astronomy fair.

The astronomy fair was a huge success. People from neighboring towns came to see the exhibits, participate in interactive workshops, and listen to Luna's captivating talks about the mysteries of the universe. It was a day of celebration, not just of astronomy, but of individuality and following one's heart.

One evening, while Luna was setting up her telescope outside her home, a little girl from the neighborhood approached her. "I want to be like you, Luna," the girl said shyly. "I love the stars too, but I'm also scared of being different."

Luna knelt down and smiled at the girl. "Being different is what makes us special," she said. "Never be afraid to shine in your own way. The world needs your unique light."

As Luna grew up, her journey took her to many places. She visited observatories, attended international conferences, and even helped develop educational programs to inspire the next generation of astronomers. Her love for astronomy remained a beacon, guiding her on a path filled with discovery and wonder.

Luna never forgot her roots in Melodyvale. She often returned to her beloved town, sharing her experiences and encouraging young minds to pursue their passions. She became a role model, not just for aspiring astronomers, but for anyone who ever felt different or out of place.

Years later, Luna achieved one of her biggest dreams. She was part of a team that built a new observatory on the outskirts of Melodyvale. The observatory became a center of learning and discovery, attracting people from all walks of life. Luna's dream of bringing the stars closer to people had come true.

At the observatory's opening ceremony, Luna looked at the crowd gathered, her heart swelling with joy. She saw faces full of curiosity and wonder, gazing up at the night sky through the telescopes.

In that moment, Luna realized the true impact of her journey. She had not only followed her own path but had also lit the way for others to discover and embrace their true selves.

Luna's True Melody

"Be true to oneself," Luna shared in her opening speech, "and you'll find the universe opening its arms to you in ways you never imagined. Our differences, our unique passions, are the stars that light up the world's sky. Let's cherish them and shine together."

And so, Luna's legacy continued, a legacy of knowledge, inspiration, and the enduring message to be true to oneself. The observatory stood as a symbol of her journey, a place where the melodies of the heart met the symphony of the stars.

The End.

This story of Luna in Melodyvale is a tender tale that inspires young girls to embrace their true passions and interests, even if they differ from those around them. It emphasizes the importance of individuality and the beauty of following one's own path.

Hannah's Artful Adventure

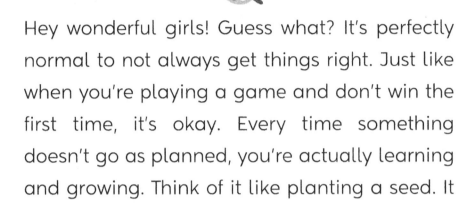

Hey wonderful girls! Guess what? It's perfectly normal to not always get things right. Just like when you're playing a game and don't win the first time, it's okay. Every time something doesn't go as planned, you're actually learning and growing. Think of it like planting a seed. It doesn't become a flower overnight, right? It takes time, sunshine, and a few rainy days.

Mistakes are like those rainy days – they help you grow stronger and smarter. So, don't worry about getting everything perfect. Just keep trying, and remember, every great person has made plenty of mistakes too.

In the colorful town of Blossom Creek, where every street was lined with blooming flowers and cheerful laughter echoed through the air, there was a young girl named Hannah. With her bright red hair and a heart full of dreams, Hannah loved nothing more than to draw and paint. Her room was a kaleidoscope of her artwork, with sketches and paintings adorning every wall.

One sunny afternoon, while Hannah was painting a picture of her cat, Whiskers, she had an idea. "I'm going to paint a mural on our garden wall!" she excitedly told her parents. Her parents loved the idea and gave her their full support.

Hannah began planning her mural. She wanted it to be a scene from her favorite storybook, a magical forest filled with colorful animals and twinkling stars. She could already imagine how beautiful it would look.

The next day, Hannah started painting the garden wall. She painted with all her heart, completely lost in her world of colors. But when she took a step back to look at her work, her heart sank. The painting didn't look anything like she had imagined. The colors seemed all wrong, the animals looked strange, and the stars didn't twinkle at all.

Feeling disappointed and a little embarrassed, Hannah wished she could just erase it all. Tears welled up in her eyes as she thought about her failed mural.

Seeing Hannah upset, her older brother, Ben, who was always there for her, came over. "Hey, what's wrong?" he asked.

Hannah sniffed, "My mural is terrible, Ben. I thought I could make something beautiful, but I just messed it up."

Feeling disappointed and a little embarrassed,

Hannah wished she could just erase it all. Tears welled up in her eyes as she thought about her failed mural.

Seeing Hannah upset, her older brother, Ben, who was always there for her, came over. "Hey, what's wrong?" he asked.

Hannah sniffed, "My mural is terrible, Ben. I thought I could make something beautiful, but I just messed it up."

Ben looked at the wall and then at Hannah. "You know, even the best artists don't always get it right the first time," he said. "What matters is that you tried. Why don't you give it another shot? Maybe plan it out a bit more this time."

Hannah wiped her tears and thought about Ben's words. He was right. She remembered her art teacher saying that making mistakes was a part of creating something beautiful.

The next day, Hannah started her mural again, this time with a clearer plan in mind. She sketched her ideas on paper before painting them on the wall. She was more careful with her colors and paid attention to the little details.

But again, when she finished, the mural didn't look as magical as she had hoped. The animals still looked odd, and the forest didn't feel enchanted.

Hannah felt like giving up. "Maybe I'm just not good at painting murals," she thought sadly.

Her mom noticed Hannah's frustration and came to talk to her. "Hannah, it's wonderful that you're trying so hard," her mom said. "But remember, it's okay if things don't turn out perfect. Every mistake is a chance to learn and improve."

Encouraged by her mom's words, Hannah decided to try one last time. She spent the next few days studying pictures of forests and animals, learning about perspective and shading. She realized that she had much to learn about painting murals.

With renewed determination, Hannah started her mural for the third time. She worked slowly, taking care to bring her magical forest to life. She painted graceful deer, wise old owls, and even a hidden fairy.

This time, when she stepped back to look at her work, a smile spread across her face. The mural was beautiful, filled with wonder and magic. It wasn't perfect, but it was hers, and she had poured her heart into it.

Hannah's family and friends gathered to see her mural. They were amazed by how much it had improved. "It's beautiful, Hannah," they exclaimed. "You've really made something special."

Hannah felt a warm glow of pride. She had faced failure, but she didn't let it stop her. Instead, she learned from her mistakes and kept trying.

Hannah's mural became a source of joy in Blossom Creek. Neighbors and passersby would stop to admire it, each finding their favorite part in the magical forest Hannah had created.

Through her journey with the mural, Hannah learned an important lesson. She learned that failure is a normal part of doing something new. It wasn't about getting it right the first time but about the learning and growing that happened along the way.

Hannah continued to paint and draw, experimenting with new ideas and techniques. Each new piece of art was a reminder of her journey – a journey filled with challenges, learning, and triumph. She knew that in each mistake lay the opportunity to become a better artist and a stronger person.

And so, Hannah kept painting, her heart full of colors and her spirit undimmed by fear of failure. She knew that in the world of art, as in life, the most beautiful stories were those filled with perseverance and the courage to try again.

The End.

In this story, Hannah's experience with painting a mural teaches young girls the valuable lesson that failure is a normal part of learning and growing. It highlights the importance of perseverance, learning from mistakes, and the joy of creative expression.

Alyssa's Choice

Always remember, inside you there's a special voice, your instincts, and they're super smart! They're like a secret guide, helping you decide what's right for you. When you have to make a choice, listen to that little nudge inside. It's like having a superhero power that helps you be the best you can be. Trusting your instincts is like trusting yourself. Sometimes others might have different ideas, and that's okay, but what you feel deep down is really important. So, be brave, listen to your heart, and let your inner superhero shine!

Alyssa's family lived in the small coastal town of Seabreeze, where the ocean sang lullabies and the sky painted dreams. Alyssa was known for her bright smile and her adventurous spirit. She had a unique talent for making friends and bringing joy to those around her.

Alyssa's family owned a quaint little bakery in the heart of Seabreeze. The bakery was famous for its delicious cakes and pastries, and Alyssa loved helping her parents there. But deep down, Alyssa harbored dreams of becoming a scientist. She was fascinated by the mysteries of the ocean and the secrets of the stars.

One day, Alyssa's school announced a special project. Each student was to present an idea that would benefit the community. The best idea would receive support and funding to make it a reality.

Alyssa's heart raced with excitement. She saw this as an opportunity to pursue her passion for science. She thought about proposing a project to clean up the local beach and protect marine life.

However, when Alyssa shared her idea with her friends, they didn't seem as enthusiastic as she had hoped. "Why not propose something about the bakery? Everyone loves your family's pastries," suggested one friend. "Maybe you could organize a bake sale for charity," said another.

Alyssa felt a twinge of doubt. Her friends' ideas made sense, and she knew everyone loved the bakery. But her heart was drawn to the beach project. She felt torn between her friends' expectations and her own aspirations.

That evening, Alyssa sat at the bakery, watching the sunset over the ocean. She thought about her friends' suggestions and her own idea. She remembered her parents always telling her, "Trust your instincts, Alyssa. They will guide you to the right path."

Alyssa realized she needed to follow her heart. She decided to go ahead with her beach clean-up and marine life protection project. She spent the next few days researching, planning, and preparing her presentation.

When the day came to present the projects, Alyssa stood in front of the class, her palms sweaty and her heart pounding. As she began to speak about the importance of protecting the marine environment and the steps they could take to clean up the beach, her nervousness faded. She spoke passionately, her voice steady and clear.

The class listened in silence, captivated by Alyssa's words and the depth of her knowledge. When she finished, there was a moment of quiet, followed by a round of applause. Alyssa's teacher, Mrs. Thompson, had a look of pride in her eyes.

The following week, the school announced that Alyssa's project had been chosen. Alyssa was overjoyed. Her project was not only recognized, but it also sparked interest among her classmates in environmental issues.

Alyssa, with the help of her friends, teachers, and some local volunteers, organized a beach clean-up day. They collected trash, learned about the local ecosystem, and even invited a marine biologist to speak about ocean conservation.

The cleanup day was a success. The beach was transformed, and everyone felt a sense of achievement and responsibility towards their environment. Alyssa's project had made a real environment. Alyssa's project had made a real difference.

Alyssa's parents were proud of her. "You followed your heart, and you made an impact," her mom said, hugging her.

Her dad added, "You trusted your instincts, Alyssa, and that's what matters."

The project was just the beginning for Alyssa. She became more involved in environmental activities, joining clubs and participating in science fairs. Her passion for science and the environment only grew stronger.

Years later, Alyssa went on to study marine biology. She became an advocate for ocean conservation, inspiring others with her dedication and love for the marine world. She often returned to Seabreeze to lead beach cleanups and educational programs.

Alyssa's choice to follow her instincts and pursue her passion for science taught her the importance of staying true to oneself. It showed her that when you listen to your heart and trust your inner voice, you can achieve great things and make a positive impact in the world.

And so, Alyssa continued to explore, learn, and protect the ocean she loved so much. Her journey was a reminder to everyone in Seabreeze, and beyond, that trusting your instincts is the key to finding your true path in life.

The End.

This story of Alyssa in Seabreeze encourages young girls to trust their instincts and follow their passions, even when it means going against expectations. It highlights the importance of staying true to oneself and the positive impact one can make by doing so.

Gracie's Heart of Gratitude

Did you know something really cool? Being thankful for what you have makes you super happy! Think about all the good stuff in your life, like your family, friends, and even your favorite toy or book. These things are super special. Sure, it's okay to wish for things, but don't forget to be happy with what you already have. Every day, try to think of a few things that make you smile and say "thank you" for them. You'll see how this little habit fills your days with lots of joy and makes you feel really lucky and happy! Remember, the best treasures are often the things you already have.

In the quaint town of Brooksville, where the streets were lined with vibrant flowers and laughter echoed from every corner, there lived a young girl named Gracie. Gracie, with her bright blue eyes and a cascade of curly brown hair, was a beacon of energy and joy. However, despite her cheerful demeanor, Gracie often found herself longing for things she didn't have. She envied her friends' bigger houses, newer toys, and family vacations to far-off places.

Gracie's family lived in a modest but cozy home, full of warmth and love. Her parents worked hard to provide for Gracie and her younger brother, Sam, but they couldn't afford many luxuries. Gracie loved her family, yet she couldn't help but wish for more.

One autumn afternoon, Gracie's teacher, Mrs. Parker, introduced the class to a new assignment called "The Gratitude Project." The task was simple: each student was to write down three things they were thankful for every day for a month. Gracie approached the assignment with little enthusiasm, unsure of what she could possibly be grateful for in her ordinary life.

That evening, as she sat at her small desk, Gracie struggled to think of something to write. She glanced around her room, her eyes landing on her favorite teddy bear, Mr. Cuddles, and then to the stack of well-loved books beside her bed. Hesitantly, she wrote, "My teddy bear, my books, and my cozy bed." It wasn't much, she thought, but it was a start.

The next day, Gracie noted, "Mom's homemade cookies, Dad's bedtime stories, and playing hide and seek with Sam." As she wrote these simple joys, a warm feeling began to stir in her heart. She was reminded of the love and care that filled her home.

With each passing day, Gracie found it easier to identify things she was grateful for. She wrote about her grandmother's funny stories, her teacher's encouraging words, and the beautiful tree outside her window that changed with the seasons.

As the days turned into weeks, a transformation began within Gracie. She started to see her life in a new light, appreciating the small moments that she had previously overlooked. The sound of her family laughing together, the smell of rain on a lazy afternoon, and the comfort of her warm, inviting home – all these things took on a new significance.

Gracie's perspective wasn't the only thing that changed. Her attitude shifted too. She became more helpful around the house, more patient with her little brother, and more understanding of her parents' hard work. Her family noticed this change and it brought them even closer together.

Inspired by her own transformation, Gracie decided to create a "Gratitude Wall" in her home. She hung a large piece of paper in the living room where each family member could write down something they were thankful for every day. The wall quickly filled with notes of gratitude, turning into a colorful tapestry of their family's blessings.

The Gratitude Wall became a cherished part of their daily routine. It was a place of reflection and appreciation, reminding them of the abundance in their lives. Gracie's parents were proud of her initiative and how it brought even more joy into their home.

Seeing the positive impact of her Gratitude Wall, Gracie decided to share the concept with her friends. She talked about it at school, explaining how it had helped her appreciate the little things in life. Her friends were inspired by her idea and started their own gratitude practices.

As Gracie continued her gratitude journey, she realized that happiness doesn't come from having everything but from appreciating everything you have. She learned that joy can be found in the simplest of things – a shared meal, a kind gesture, a beautiful sunset.

Her newfound attitude of gratitude even began to influence her classmates. Gracie's class became more harmonious, with students showing more kindness and appreciation towards each other. Mrs. Parker noticed the shift and praised Gracie for being a role model.

Encouraged by the positive changes in her life, Gracie wanted to spread the message of gratitude even further. She proposed a school-wide gratitude project, similar to her Gratitude Wall at home. With Mrs. Parker's support, the project was implemented, and soon, every classroom had its own Gratitude Wall.

The project was a resounding success, fostering a sense of community and thankfulness throughout the school. Students and teachers alike shared in this culture of gratitude, celebrating both big achievements and everyday blessings.

As the project came to a close, Mrs. Parker organized a "Gratitude Day" at school. On this day, everyone shared stories of how gratitude had impacted their lives. Gracie stood before her classmates, her heart full as she shared her journey.

"I learned that being thankful for what you have brings more happiness than longing for what you don't," Gracie said. "Gratitude has made me see how rich my life really is."

Her words resonated with her classmates, many of whom had experienced similar transformations. The Gratitude Day became an annual tradition at the school, a day to celebrate and appreciate the many gifts in each person's life.

Gracie continued to embrace gratitude every day. She found joy in the ordinary and beauty in the small moments. Her journey taught her that gratitude isn't just about being thankful; it's a way of seeing the world.

Through her example, Gracie inspired not only her family and friends but also her entire community. Her simple act of acknowledging the good in her life had a ripple effect, spreading positivity and contentment to those around her.

As Gracie grew older, she carried the lesson of gratitude with her, allowing it to guide her through life's challenges and triumphs. She knew that no matter where life took her, she would always find something to be thankful for.

The End.

In this story, Gracie's journey of discovering gratitude in the small joys of life teaches young girls the importance of being thankful for everything they have. It highlights how an attitude of gratitude can positively transform one's outlook and spread happiness to others.

Alexa at the Old Mansion

It's super cool to be brave and try new things, right? Taking risks can lead you to amazing adventures and help you discover just how strong and capable you are. But, it's also really important to think about what could happen. Just like when you're about to jump into a pool, you make sure it's safe first, right? So, whenever you're ready to leap into something new, take a moment to think about the consequences. This way, you can have all the fun and excitement while staying safe and smart. Remember, being brave also means being wise!

Alexa is a young adventurous girl who lived with her parents in the bustling town of Cloverfield, where every corner was filled with friendly faces and children's laughter. With her spirited nature and a head full of dreams, Alexa was always ready for a new adventure. She was fearless, often leading her friends in exciting escapades. But sometimes, her bravery led her to make hasty decisions without thinking about what could happen later.

Alexa's parents encouraged her boldness but often reminded her, "It's great to be brave, Alexa, but remember to think things through. Every choice has a consequence, so be careful."

On a gloomy Saturday, Alexa and her friends discovered an old, abandoned mansion at the edge of Cloverfield. The mansion, with its peeling paint and overgrown garden, had been the center of many spooky local tales. Curiosity got the better of them, and despite their parents' warnings to stay away, they decided to explore it.

As they approached the mansion, Alexa felt a thrill of excitement. The mansion stood silent, its windows like dark, mysterious eyes. Her friends were hesitant, but Alexa, eager to explore, stepped forward confidently. "Come on, it'll be an adventure!" she exclaimed.

Inside, the house was eerie yet fascinating. Dusty furniture lay untouched, and shadows danced on the walls. They wandered through the rooms on the ground floor, their footsteps echoing in the silence.

Feeling bolder, Alexa suggested they explore upstairs. Despite their reservations, her friends followed, drawn by both the mystery and Alexa's infectious enthusiasm.

As they ascended the creaky staircase, Alexa was in the lead, her curiosity overshadowing her caution. The thrill of exploration was all she could think about. But she didn't notice the weakened steps, worn by time and neglect.

Suddenly, there was a loud crack. One of the steps collapsed under Alexa's foot, and she stumbled, trying to regain her balance. Her heart raced as she grabbed the railing, narrowly avoiding a fall. Her friends gasped in shock, rushing to her aid.

For a moment, they all stood there, hearts pounding, the reality of what could have happened sinking in. The excitement of their adventure had almost led to a dangerous fall. The risks they had ignored in their eagerness to explore were now glaringly apparent.

Alexa looked at her friends, their faces a mix of fear and relief. "I'm sorry," she said, her voice shaky. "I should have listened and been more careful. We could have gotten really hurt."

The group carefully made their way back down-stairs, supporting each other as they went. The fun and thrill they had felt earlier were replaced by a sobering realization of the potential dangers they had ignored.

Once outside, Alexa took a deep breath of fresh air, grateful that everyone was safe. The old house, once an emblem of adventure, now stood as a reminder of the fine line between bravery and recklessness.

The walk back home was quiet, each of them lost in their thoughts. Alexa replayed the incident in her mind, realizing how her impulsive decision could have led to serious consequences. She thought about her parents' advice and understood what they meant about thinking things through.

Back home, Alexa shared the day's events with her parents. They were concerned but relieved that no one was hurt. "Alexa, we're proud of you for recognizing the risk and for taking responsibility," her mom said, hugging her.

Her dad added, "Being adventurous is good, but being safe is important too. It's about finding the right balance."

The experience at the old house was a turning point for Alexa. She learned an important lesson about risk-taking and the importance of being mindful of potential dangers. She realized that true bravery wasn't about diving headfirst into every situation but about knowing when to take a step back and assess the risks.

From that day on, Alexa approached her adventures with a new perspective. She still led her friends on exciting escapades, but now she made sure they were safe and thought out. She became an example of responsible bravery to her peers.

The incident at the old house became a story that Alexa often reflected on. It reminded her of the valuable lesson she had learned - that being brave also means being wise and considerate of the consequences of one's actions.

In Cloverfield, Alexa's story became a lesson for other children too. Her experience showed that while adventures are exciting, being cautious and aware is equally important. It encouraged other kids to think twice before stepping into uncertain situations and to value safety along with fun.

Alexa's journey taught her the significance of balancing her adventurous spirit with a sense of responsibility. This balance became her new way of life, guiding her in making decisions that were both brave and thoughtful.

The End.

Alexa's story emphasizes the importance of thinking ahead and understanding the risks involved in any adventurous endeavor. It teaches young girls that while being adventurous and courageous is admirable, being aware of the consequences and ensuring safety is crucial.

Maggie's Day of Giving

Girls, you know, you don't need a special title or award to be incredible. You're already awesome just by being you! Whether you're the fastest runner, the smartest in class, or just being your wonderful self, it's all super cool. What really matters is how kind, brave, and caring you are. Your actions, your smiles, and your kindness make you special. So, don't worry if you don't have a fancy title. Just being the amazing you is more than enough.

The story took place at the lively town of Greenfield, where every street was bustling with life and joy. With her cheerful demeanor and a heart full of kindness, Maggie was just the same with any other girl in town. She wasn't known as the smartest in her class, the fastest on the track team, or the most popular; she was just Maggie, and sometimes she felt that wasn't enough.

Maggie's parents always told her, "You are special just being you, Maggie. Remember, it's not the titles that define you, but your actions and your kindness."

Greenfield was preparing for its much-anticipated annual event, the Community Day Fair. This year, the theme was "Unsung Heroes" – a tribute to those who contribute to the community in their own quiet, significant ways. Maggie loved the idea and eagerly wanted to participate. But she struggled to find where she fit in among the more noticeable talents and roles of others.

As the fair day approached, Maggie decided to volunteer without a specific role, simply offering help wherever it was needed. The morning of the fair, she arrived early, her heart racing with excitement and a bit of nervousness.

Maggie's first task was at the welcoming booth, greeting people with her warm, inviting smile. She handed out brochures and guided visitors, her pleasant demeanor making everyone feel at ease.

Next, she helped at the games section, cheering on the kids and helping to organize the activities. Her laughter and energy were infectious, and soon more children flocked to the games area, their giggles and cheers filling the air.

As the day went on, Maggie found herself doing various tasks – from assisting at the food stands to helping the elderly find their way around. Her presence became a constant throughout the fair, her helpfulness and cheerful nature not going unnoticed.

While Maggie was busy assisting at a craft booth, there was a little girl, who had come to the fair with her family, got separated from her parents. She was scared and began to cry amidst the crowd. Maggie noticed her and immediately went to comfort her.

"Poor little baby, you must be lost out here! What's your name?" Maggie asked. "Lily." the little girl shyly replied.

"It's going to be okay, Lily. I'm here with you, and we'll find your parents," Maggie said, kneeling beside the frightened girl. She took Lily's hand and began to look around for her parents, all the while keeping Lily calm with her gentle words.

With Maggie's help, they soon found Lily's grateful parents, who thanked Maggie profusely for her kindness and quick action. Maggie simply smiled and said, "I'm just glad I could help."

As the fair came to an end, the mayor of Greenfield took to the stage to give a speech. He spoke about the importance of community and how everyone, in their own way, contributes to the town's spirit. He then announced a special recognition for an "Unsung Hero" – someone who had shown exceptional kindness and helpfulness throughout the day.

To Maggie's surprise, the mayor called her name. "Maggie, please come up to the stage. Today, you have shown us what it truly means to be an 'Unsung Hero.' Your kindness, your willingness to help, and your cheerful spirit have made a significant difference."

Maggie walked up to the stage, her cheeks flushed with a mix of surprise and joy. The applause from the crowd was overwhelming. She realized that her small acts of kindness throughout the day had not gone unnoticed.

The mayor presented Maggie with a small trophy, a symbol of appreciation and recognition. "Maggie, you may not hold a formal title, but today, you have shown that you are a hero in your own right," the mayor said.

Standing on the stage, trophy in hand, Maggie looked out at the crowd. She saw smiling faces, some familiar, some new, all celebrating her. At that moment, Maggie understood what her parents had always told her – that it was not about having a title, but about the impact of her actions and the kindness she shared.

After the fair, Maggie continued to volunteer and help in her community, always with the same enthusiasm and love. She had learned that being an "Unsung Hero" was about doing small things with great love, and that was something she could do every day.

From that day on, Maggie never again doubted her worth or her place in the world. She knew that she had her own special way of making a difference, and that was more than enough.

The End.

In this story, Maggie learns that a title or a specific role doesn't define her worth or her ability to make a positive impact. She discovers that her value lies in her actions, kindness, and the willingness to help others, transcending the need for formal recognition or titles.

Niki's Blooming Miracle

❊❊❊

Did you know that one of the best things you can do is giving love freely? It's like sharing a piece of your heart with the world. When you show kindness, help others, or just give a big smile, you're spreading love. And the coolest part? This love doesn't cost a thing, yet it's super valuable. It can make someone's day brighter or even change their whole world. So, don't be afraid to be generous with your love. It's a superpower that makes you and everyone around you happier.

Niki was a little girl living in the endearing town of Meadowbrook, where every path was a tapestry of kindness and support. Niki, who was well-known for her gentle nature and her beaming smile, held a particular conviction: love should be given freely and without conditions. Niki had always been taught by her mother that: "Love is a gift. Giving it freely allows it to flourish and makes everyone happy."

One day, while walking past the edge of town, Niki noticed Mrs. Jenkins' once beautiful garden, now wilted and neglected. Mrs. Jenkins, a sweet elderly lady, had recently fallen ill and could no longer tend to her beloved garden. Niki remembered how Mrs. Jenkins' garden used to be the pride of Meadowbrook, its blooms a vibrant splash of color that brought smiles to everyone who passed by.

A thought struck Niki. She wanted to bring back the joy that Mrs. Jenkins' garden had once given to the community. Excitedly, Niki shared her idea with her friends – they would restore Mrs. Jenkins' garden to its former glory as a surprise.

The children gathered their gardening tools and set to work. They weeded the overgrown patches, planted new flowers, and watered the parched soil. They even painted stones in bright, cheerful colors to line the garden paths. Each child poured their love into every task, thinking of Mrs. Jenkins' smile when she would see her revived garden.

Word of their project spread through Meadowbrook, and soon, neighbors began to contribute. Some brought flowers and plants, others offered gardening tips, and some brought lemonade and snacks for the hardworking children. It was incredible to see how a simple act of kindness from Niki had sparked a wave of generosity throughout the town.

Meanwhile, Niki spent time with Mrs. Jenkins, keeping her company and sharing little updates about the town and their daily lives, careful not to reveal the surprise. Mrs. Jenkins enjoyed these visits, finding comfort and joy in Niki's stories and laughter.

After several days of diligent work, the garden was transformed. The once dull and forlorn space now burst with life and color. Roses, daisies, sunflowers, and lilies smiled at the sun, and the air was fragrant with the scent of fresh blooms.

The day arrived to reveal the surprise to Mrs. Jenkins. The children led her into the garden, her eyes covered with a gentle blindfold. When they finally removed it, Mrs. Jenkins stood in awe. Tears welled up in her eyes as she gazed at the blooming miracle before her.

"This is the most beautiful thing anyone has ever done for me," Mrs. Jenkins whispered, her voice trembling with emotion. "Thank you, my dears. Thank you for bringing my garden, my joy, back to life."

The children, seeing the impact of their work, felt a deep sense of fulfillment. They had not only revived a garden but had also rekindled the spirit of love and community in Meadowbrook.

The mayor of Meadowbrook, having heard of the children's project, visited the garden. He was deeply moved by their act of kindness and the beauty they had created. "You children have done something remarkable," he said. "You've shown us all the power of giving love freely. Your work here goes beyond just gardening; you've sown seeds of love and kindness in Meadow-brook."

Niki, standing among her friends and the blooming flowers, felt her heart swell with pride and joy. She realized that love, when given freely, has the power to create wonders and bring a community together.

From that day forward, Mrs. Jenkins' garden became a symbol of Meadowbrook's unity and compassion. Neighbors took turns helping to maintain the garden, making it a collective labor of love. Mrs. Jenkins, rejuvenated by the love

Niki's Blooming Miracle

shown to her, often sat in her garden, sharing stories and wisdom with those who visited.

Niki continued to embody the spirit of generosity, always looking for ways to spread love and kindness. Her belief in giving love freely had transformed not just a garden, but the hearts of those around her.

The story of Niki and Mrs. Jenkins' garden spread throughout Meadowbrook, inspiring others to open their hearts and extend their hands in love and service. The town, already a close-knit community, grew even closer, bonded by the shared experience of creating something beautiful out of love and kindness.

Niki's simple yet profound act of love had shown everyone in Meadowbrook that the most significant gifts often come not from material things, but from the heart. And in Meadowbrook, hearts were always full, and love was always in bloom. *The End*

In this story, Niki's initiative to restore Mrs. Jenkins' garden becomes a communal act of love, illustrating the lesson of giving love freely and the transformative power it holds. This story aims to inspire young girls to understand the impact of kindness and the beauty of selfless love.

Zoe's Ascent to the Stars

★★★

Did you know that you have the power to achieve anything you dream of? Yes, you! Whether you want to be a scientist, an artist, or even an astronaut, you can do it. Sometimes things might seem tough, and you might face challenges, but remember, these are just steps on your journey to success. Believe in yourself, work hard, and never give up on your dreams. You are strong, smart, and capable of amazing things. So go ahead, chase those dreams, and remember, you can do anything you set your mind to.

Living amid verdant meadows and soft hills was a girl named Zoe in the peaceful village of Willow Creek. With a heart full of dreams, Zoe was renowned for her endless vitality. There was something special and distinct in her eyes, a sparkle that conveyed her desire to do great things. Her favorite saying, taught by her grandmother, was, "Zoe, remember, you can do anything you set your mind to. Just believe and persevere."

Zoe was fascinated by the majestic mountain that stood at the edge of Willow Creek. Towering over the landscape, it was a giant, its peak lost in the clouds. Zoe dreamt of climbing that mountain, a dream that seemed outlandish to many in her small town.

Whenever she shared her dream, she received mixed reactions. While her friends admired her courage, others doubted, saying, "It's too risky, Zoe. It's not something for young girls." These words stung, but Zoe refused to let them dim her dream.

Zoe's Ascent to the Stars

Determined to turn her dream into reality, Zoe started preparing with unwavering dedication. She read books on mountaineering, practiced on smaller hills, and worked on building her strength and endurance. Her parents, seeing her determination, supported her with the right gear and guidance.

Zoe's training was rigorous. With each passing day, she grew stronger, both physically and mentally. The journey was tough, filled with challenges that tested her limits, but Zoe's resolve only grew stronger.

Finally, the day arrived when Zoe felt ready to face the mountain. With a backpack filled with essentials and a heart full of determination, she set off before dawn. The mountain stood tall against the morning sky, its peak glowing with the first light of day.

The climb was arduous. The path was steep, filled with treacherous turns and loose stones. Zoe faced each obstacle with grit, remembering her grandmother's words. Her muscles ached, and her breath grew heavy, but her spirit did not waver.

As she ascended, doubts crept into her mind. The whispers of discouragement she had heard echoed in her thoughts. There were moments when Zoe wondered if she had embarked on an impossible journey. But with each step upward, she pushed these doubts away, focusing on her goal.

The higher Zoe climbed, the more challenging the journey became. The air thinned, and the terrain grew rugged. Zoe had to rely on all her skills and knowledge. Every step required focus and determination.

Hours passed, and Zoe continued her ascent. Her body was weary, but her resolve was unbreakable. She remembered why she had started this journey – to follow her dream and to show that anything is possible if you believe in yourself.

Finally, after what seemed like an eternity, Zoe reached the summit. She stood there, at the top of the world, her eyes wide with wonder and her heart overflowing with triumph. She had done it. She had climbed the mountain that many thought was impossible for her to conquer.

From the peak, the view was breathtaking. The world below looked like a beautiful painting, a tapestry of colors and life. But more beautiful than the view was the feeling of accomplishment that swelled in Zoe's heart.

As Zoe descended back to Willow Creek, she was not just a girl who had climbed a mountain. She was a symbol of courage, a living proof that dreams can be achieved with belief and hard work.

When she returned, Zoe was greeted with admiration and awe. Her story of conquering the mountain spread through Willow Creek, inspiring everyone, especially young girls who had dreams of their own.

Zoe's journey taught her the power of self-belief and perseverance. She learned that the path to achieving your dreams might be filled with challenges, but it's the courage to continue that truly matters.

Zoe continued to chase her dreams, each new challenge a mountain of its own. But with her ascent to the peak of the mountain, she had shown not just herself, but everyone in Willow Creek, that with determination and faith, you truly can do anything.

In the heart of Willow Creek, Zoe's story became a beacon of inspiration, a reminder that no dream is too big, and no mountain too high, for a heart filled with courage and a spirit ready to soar.

The End.

In this extended version, Zoe's journey to climb the mountain serves as an inspiring metaphor for overcoming obstacles and achieving one's dreams. It teaches young girls the importance of believing in themselves and the power of perseverance in reaching their goals.

Made in the USA
Monee, IL
03 November 2024

69202627R00050